discard

GALÁPAGOS

BY
Maxine McCormick
& Phyllis Root

The authors wish to thank Adela Elwell, biologist, Claude Riedel, and Kristen Nelson for all their help. Any mistakes are our own.

CRESTWOOD HOUSE
New York

LIBRARY OF CONGRESS CATALOGING IN PUBLICATION DATA

McCormick, Maxine.
  Galápagos / by Maxine McCormick and Phyllis Root
  p. cm.—(National parks)

  Includes index.
  SUMMARY: Describes the geography, history, and plant and animal life of the Galápagos Islands.
  1. Natural history—Galápagos Islands—Juvenile literature. 2. Galápagos Islands—Description and travel—Juvenile literature.
  [1. Galápagos Islands. 2. National parks and reserves.] I. Root, Phyllis. II. Title. III. Series: National parks
  QH198.G3R66   1989   508.866'5—dc20   89-7918
  ISBN 0-89686-434-0   CIP
                                                                                AC

PHOTO CREDITS

Cover: FPG International: Jeffrey Sylvester
DRK Photo: (D. Cavagnaro) 4, 24, 28, 31, 36; (Kim Heacox) 34; (M. P. Kahl) 35
FPG International: (Carl Roessler) 7; (Myron Sutton) 8, 22; (Jeffrey Sylvester) 15; (Dario Sacramone) 12, 17; (E. Manewal) 18, 21; (Keith Gunnar) 32
Claude Riedel: 11, 25, 27, 29, 37, 38, 42-43

Copyright © 1989 by CRESTWOOD HOUSE, Macmillan Publishing Company

All rights reserved. No part of this book may be reproduced or transmitted in any form or by any means, electronic or mechanical, including photocopying, recording, or by any information storage and retrieval system, without permission in writing from the Publisher.

Macmillan Publishing Company
866 Third Avenue
New York, NY 10022
Collier Macmillan Canada, Inc.

Produced by Carnival Enterprises

Printed in the United States

First Edition

10 9 8 7 6 5 4 3 2 1

TABLE OF CONTENTS

The Enchanted Islands... 5
Where Did the Islands Come from?... 6
How Big? How Wide? How Many?... 9
By Sea and By Air... 9
Finding a Niche... 10
Visitors... 13
Discovery... 13
Buccaneers, Pirates, and Whalers... 15
Prisoners and Colonists... 16
A Scientist Arrives... 19
The Desert in the Sea... 19
Giant Cacti and Sunflower Trees... 20
"Walking Stones"... 23
Sea Dragons... 25
The Chilly Tropics... 26
Islands of Birds... 29
Darwin's Finches... 30
Life in a Caldera... 32
Dance of the Blue-Footed Booby... 33
Pirates of the Skies... 35
Life at the Water's Edge... 37
Dangers and Damages... 39
Saving the Islands... 40
For More Park Information... 44
Park Map... 45
Glossary/Index... 46-47

Galápagos National Park

South America

THE ENCHANTED ISLANDS

The Galápagos Islands exploded out of the sea more than a million years ago. These islands are actually the tops of huge ocean volcanoes.

As the hot islands cooled, plants and animals from South America began to arrive. Many died. They could not survive on an island with little soil and little water. Those that did survive evolved into strange and wonderful creatures.

Six-hundred-pound, cactus-eating tortoises lumber slowly along. They are so large they look like walking stones or little armored tanks. Sunflowers have grown into 60-foot trees. Birds with brilliant blue feet dance and dive. Foot-long centipedes hide in the rocks. Penguins splash feet-first into the surf, braying like donkeys.

Marine iguanas live here and nowhere else. They look like small dragons. To survive they eat seaweed and drink the salty ocean water.

If you are walking along the crest of a volcano, a mockingbird or a tiny finch may land on your shoulder. Because the Galápagos are so isolated, the creatures have little or no fear of people.

The Galápagos sit on the equator, halfway between the north and south poles, 600 miles west of South America. Pink flamingoes and

The huge tortoise is one of the many rare animals that make their homes in Galápagos National Park.

penguins live on different parts of these islands. One is a tropical bird, and the other is from the land of ice and snow. How can penguins from cold southern waters live on the equator?

Charles Darwin visited these islands in 1835. He realized they were special. Many strange plants and animals lived there and nowhere else. It was Darwin who brought these amazing islands to the world's attention.

Today the Galápagos Islands are a national park. They are a gift from the people of Ecuador for all the world to preserve and respect.

WHERE DID THE ISLANDS COME FROM?

Millions of years ago the islands began to grow on the bottom of the sea. Out of a *hot spot*, a huge crack beneath the ocean floor, hot molten *magma* (liquid rock) was forced upwards. Strong ocean currents carried the *lava* outward and spread it over the sea floor. Layer piled upon layer, building a large, broad platform. On top of this platform rose the volcanoes.

Then one day the top of one of the volcanoes poked through the surface of the water. Hot liquid rock shot out from below the waves. The ocean boiled and thundered from the tremendous heat and pressure. Upward and upward the island grew as lava was blown from deep below the ocean floor. Today the tallest volcano islands rise up to 5,000 feet above the sea.

Scientists think the oldest islands may be four million years old. But most are between one and three million years old. That may sound very ancient to you, but these are considered fresh, young islands—one of the most active volcano groups in the world. Today the roar of the volcano is still possible in the Galápagos. But mostly lava simply oozes out of cracks and *vents* and pours down the sides of the volcanoes.

Isabela, the largest island, is made of five towering volcanoes and the remains of a sixth. Over time their lavas flowed together to form one large island. Some of Isabela's volcanoes are still active. As the

FUN FACT On February 14, 1825, Benjamin Morrell, aboard the *Tartar*, witnessed the eruption of the volcano on Fernandina Island. The temperature of the water went from 61 degrees to 150 degrees Fahrenheit after two days. Sailors fainted from the heat.

lava oozes out and hardens, new rock is added to the island. So Isabela is still growing.

Most of the islands have only one volcano. Most of the volcanoes are not active.

Not all the islands in the Galápagos are the tops of volcanoes. Some are made from the lava platform that lies beneath the waves. Hot molten magma flowing beneath the sea has forced blocks of the lava platform to crack and move upwards.

On a misty morning, steam may drift up from vents in a volcano. This is called a *fumarole*. As rainwater leaks into cracks and meets hot rock deep below, it rises as hot steam. This indicates that hot magma may lie deep within.

To someone sailing by the island the volcano may appear to be ready to explode. But all is well.

Millions of years ago, the islands of the Galápagos began forming on the bottom of the sea.

Sally Lightfoot crabs decorate the shores of Española, one of the many islands that make up the Galápagos.

HOW BIG? HOW WIDE? HOW MANY?

The Galápagos are a group of 13 larger islands, 6 smaller islands, and over 40 *islets*, rocks, and reefs. Many have not been named. Isabela, by far the largest, is 75 miles long. It is bigger than all the other islands put together.

The Galápagos volcanoes are called *shield volcanoes*. They are large, low-rounded domes made up of layers of *basaltic lava*. Most measure 10 to 20 miles across the base. From a distance they resemble the giant tortoises for which the islands are famous.

In all there are more than 2,000 *craters*, large and small. Volcan Wolf, on Isabela, is the tallest volcano. It towers 5,400 feet above the ocean. Sierra Negra, another volcano on Isabela, has the largest crater. It measures about six miles across. The volcano on Fernandina Island has the deepest crater — it drops 2,700 feet from the top of its *summit*.

In June 1968, the Fernandina crater, or *caldera,* suddenly began to drop. Over a nine-day period the caldera fell 75 times, making a deeper and deeper hole in its center. On one day alone, 200 separate earthquakes shook the area. In all, it fell about 1,000 feet. Rocks crashed and tumbled within the crater. The air became clouded with dust and gases from the volcano. The lake that sat in one part of the caldera fell intact but ran to the other side. The water became so hot it killed the tiny plants and animals in the lake. The ducks that lived in or near the water died, too.

BY SEA AND BY AIR

When the first steaming islands poked through the sea, nothing grew on the bare, black lava. No birds called. No animals crawled. Every living thing on the islands had to come across at least 600 miles of open sea.

How did they come? Currents flow past these islands from the coasts of South, Central, and North America. These currents are like

FUN FACT The rice rat of the Galápagos holds the world's record for the longest ocean crossing by a land mammal.

great rivers of water flowing in the ocean. Sea lions, sea turtles, seals, and penguins are all good swimmers. They probably swam along these currents to the islands.

Some animals rode to the islands on logs or giant "rafts." These rafts form when heavy rains tear away huge chunks of earth, trees, and plants from the river banks. As the rafts are swept to the sea, animals can be caught in the floods, clinging to the tangled branches. Most of these rafts sink in the ocean. But some have been seen hundreds of miles from shore. A few rafts must have drifted safely to the Galápagos. Plants, seeds, insects, snails, iguanas, rats, snakes, and lizards could have been carried to a new island home.

Seabirds probably flew to the islands. Land birds and bats might have been blown there by winds from the mainlands. The wind brought many small, light seeds, too. Sticky or bristly seeds probably stuck to the feathers and feet of birds. Some seeds were even carried in the birds' stomachs.

Slowly, over thousands of years, life arrived.

What came first? No one knows for sure. Sea birds, sea lions, and seals eat fish and rest or nest on bare ground. They could survive when the islands were still bare, hard rock.

Lichens were probably some of the first plants on the Galápagos. They can grow on bare rock and help to change it into soil. Over time the lichens, the rain, the wind, and the sea wore the lava into soil so other plants could grow.

In turn, these plants became food for the iguanas and tortoises that floated to the islands. Birds like hawks and owls probably arrived later. They could not survive without small animals to eat.

FINDING A NICHE

It was a long, hard journey to the islands. *Reptiles* like lizards and turtles could live a long time at sea without fresh water to drink. There are many reptiles on the islands. But large *mammals*, like jaguars, could not survive such a voyage under a burning sun without food or water. Bats and rice rats are the only land mammals that reached the islands and survived.

Like other birds and animals of the Galápagos, the swallow-tailed gull has found its niche.

The seeds and animals that landed safely still faced a huge challenge. The soil on the islands was thin, the climate harsh. Food was scarce, and water scarcer. If a seed washed ashore onto hard lava or fell from the air into the ocean, it would not grow. A lizard crawling ashore from a floating log needed plants or insects to eat. Even if the lizard found food, it still needed to find a mate that had washed ashore on the same island at the same time.

Plants that survived found water and soil in cracks of the rocks. Many animals found food, water, mates, and a place to live. Slowly they spread out over the rocky land. They found or made *niches* for themselves on the islands where they could survive. Some animals may have fought each other for the same food, but others moved into niches where they did not compete.

Three kinds of birds called boobies live on the islands. Blue-footed boobies dive for fish near the shores of the islands. Red-footed boobies fish farther out to sea. Masked boobies usually hunt for food in the waters between the islands. Each bird has found its own niche.

Lava gulls on the islands feed by day, like most gulls. But the swallow-tailed gull flies out and feeds at night. Its huge eyes help it spot squid on the surface of the sea. This gull is the only gull in the world that feeds at night.

There are few kinds of trees on the islands. Most tree seeds could not survive the long voyage. But other plants have taken their place. In the dry lowlands and on the lower islands, prickly pear cacti grow as tall as trees. In the dense, damp highlands, "sunflower" plants have grown as high as 60 feet tall.

Over thousands of years these plants and animals have had to

Many of the plants found on the Galápagos Islands are not found anywhere else in the world. These plants have changed and adapted to their island home.

change, or adapt, to survive in their new island home. Many are found nowhere else in the world. If their islands change, they might not survive. They cannot ride the ocean back to the mainland. The currents do not flow that way. Even if they could, they would no longer fit into the world they left. They have changed too much. That is the price they pay for fitting so neatly into special niches.

VISITORS

The *Inca* people of South America tell a story. Around the year 1485 one of their greatest kings, Inca Tupac Yupanqui, set sail on a bold expedition. He ordered a huge fleet of balsa rafts with sails to be built. (It is known that the Incas could build such rafts.) The king and 20,000 of his best soldiers set sail on the great Mamacocha, "mother of lakes." That is the name the Incas gave the Pacific South Sea. They were gone for nearly a year.

Upon returning, it is told he brought back "black people, gold, a chair made of brass, and the skin and jawbone of a horse." He discovered two islands, which he called Ava Chumbi (Outer Island) and Nina Chumbi (Island of Fire).

It is certain that people, horses, gold, or chairs could not be found in the Galápagos. Perhaps the king raided a village elsewhere. Or perhaps he sailed farther into the Pacific Ocean than even he imagined.

But the two islands he discovered may have been part of the Galápagos. Such a fleet sent out from Peru or Ecuador would very likely reach the islands. Perhaps the "island of fire" was an active volcano and the other was an island near to it in the Galápagos.

If the Inca did come to the Galápagos, they did the islands no harm.

DISCOVERY

On February 23, 1535, the bishop of Panama, Tomas de Berlanga, set sail for Peru. He had been sent by the Emperor of Spain to settle a fight that had broken out between two leaders of the Spanish army.

FUN FACT The red-footed booby lays only one egg. Because it fishes many miles out at sea, the bird cannot get back to feed more than one chick.

It was this army that had conquered Peru and the Inca empire.

For the first week the ship kept close to the coast. But as it neared the equator, the wind died completely. The sails of the ship hung limp. The ship was becalmed at sea. This meant that the captain could not control his boat. There was no wind to fill the sails.

But the strong ocean current did not let the boat sit still. It drifted farther and farther from shore. For more than a week the sailors were powerless, caught in the grip of the strong moving current. No wind stirred. The land disappeared. Food and water ran low. The hot sun beat down on them. They feared they would be lost forever.

Finally on March 10 the crew spotted land. At last! Here was an island where they could find food and water. As the sailors neared the island, pulled by the powerful currents, they were filled with despair. All they could see was bare, black lava, heaped and strewn with stones, on which a few cacti grew.

The crew went ashore to find water to drink and grass for the horses. They came back saying that "they found nothing but seals and turtles, and such big tortoises that each could carry a man on its back, and many iguanas that are like serpents." To survive they ate the pads of prickly pear cacti. They squeezed out the juice and drank it, although it tasted bad.

Finally the sailors found water. They filled eight *hogsheads* and barrels and jugs. Still, two men and ten horses died.

They saw birds so tame the men thought them silly. But this was true of all the animals on the islands—they were not afraid of people.

In those days hundreds of thousands of tortoises lived on the islands. The Spaniards were amazed by these animals, and they named the islands after them. The name "Insulae de los Galopegos" (which means "Islands of the Tortoises") was first put on a map in 1574. But soon after the islands were known by another name.

The sailors called them the Enchanted Islands because they thought the islands were bewitched. They thought the islands floated about and could appear or disappear without warning. The sailors were terrified of the spot on the sea where the winds suddenly died, leaving them to drift helplessly for days. They feared the powerful currents that could smash their boats against the rocks.

FUN FACT Buccaneer Cove was a hideout for pirates. They once captured a cargo of eight tons of English marmalade stored in pottery jars and for years afterwards ate it there.

The Galápagos prickly pear cacti can grow as tall as trees.

BUCCANEERS, PIRATES, AND WHALERS

For 300 years the Spaniards avoided the islands. But English *pirates* and *buccaneers* had other ideas.

In the 17th century English buccaneers were sent by their king to make war on the Spanish *galleons* that carried gold from the coast of South America. Stories were told of captured gold buried on some of the Galápagos islands. But none was ever found. The English used the Galápagos as a hideout. They would attack a gold-bearing ship, then hide in the islands to divide up the booty, repair their ships, and try to find water—if they were lucky. They found the huge Galápagos tortoises a handy supply of fresh meat.

After the pirates, the whalers came. They hunted whales for their oil. Oil was needed as factories and industry grew in America and England. It was used as a fuel for lamps and as a lubricant for tools and machines. Between 1811 and 1844, at least 700 American whaling ships hunted in the Pacific. There were ships from other countries, too. They all stopped at the Galápagos for a supply of tortoises.

One ship could hold up to 500 or 600 living tortoises. They could live for as long as a year without food or water. They were a good supply of meat in the days when there was no refrigeration. For the sailors, such food was a welcome change from their usual salt pork and biscuits. The tortoises were stacked alive, one on top of the other, in the ship's hold. They were brought out and slaughtered as needed.

At this time seal hunters came, too. They hunted the fur seals for their thick, furry skins. The seals were not afraid of people. The hunters had only to walk up to the animals and club them to death. In this way, tens of thousands of Galápagos fur seals were killed.

By the end of the Civil War the whalers had stopped using the Galápagos. Oil had been discovered in America, and some species of whales were almost *extinct*. But by this time, more than 100,000 tortoises had been killed.

PRISONERS AND COLONISTS

Horror stories tell of shipwrecked sailors marooned on the Galápagos Islands. Some managed to live because they ate cactus pads or drank the blood of seals. Others perished and were never found again. For hundreds of years sailors believed these islands were impossible to live on because of their lack of water.

The first person to live on the Galápagos was an Irishman named Patrick Watkins in the early 1800s. Captain Porter of the *Essex* described him as wearing "ragged clothes...and covered with vermin; his red hair and beard matted, his skin much burnt, from...the sun,

FUN FACT In Post Office Bay is a barrel that sailors used for a mailbox. Sailors left letters in the barrels for other ships to carry to England and the United States.

In the early 1800s, a shipwrecked sailor managed to live on Floreana, one of the Galápagos Islands.

and so wild and savage...that he struck everyone with horror."

He managed to survive for several years on Floreana Island. He grew pumpkins and potatoes and other vegetables. He sold them to the whaling ships.

But most people never made it past the miles and miles of desolate lava fields that spread out around the volcanoes. This desert area is intensely hot. Farther inland on the higher islands are forest areas that are intensely wet. Both places are almost impossible to live in.

On February 12, 1832, Ecuador claimed the Galápagos as part of their country. A settlement was started on Floreana. A section of forest was cleared. Maize, sugar cane, sweet potatoes, bananas, and citrus fruits were planted. Cattle, horses, pigs, and donkeys were brought, too.

Most of the settlers were imprisoned soldiers who had been condemned to death. The prisoners were treated as slaves. Finally they rebelled and fled. The animals escaped into the wild. Several times people tried to colonize the islands, but each attempt ended in violence and murder.

In the early 1900s people brought large cattle herds to graze on the slopes of the volcano Sierra Negra on Isabela. In the 1920s a large group of Norwegian *colonists* came to settle on Santa Cruz. These families were ill-prepared to survive in this harsh land. Within a year many died. Almost all the survivors returned to their homeland.

A few stayed. Slowly more people joined them. Villages grew. Families made their livings by farming or fishing. They exported coffee, fish, and cattle. Today thousands of people make their homes in small villages scattered on four islands.

A fishing boat works quietly by the shores of Santa Cruz Island.

A SCIENTIST ARRIVES

Charles Darwin came to the islands on September 15, 1835. He was only 22 years old. He came from England on the HMS *Beagle*. His ship was on a five-year scientific mission to study many places in the world. He had come on this voyage as the ship's *naturalist*.

As Darwin walked about the islands he saw many strange things. Animals and plants on the islands were different from those on the mainland of South America. He collected specimens of animals and samples of plants.

Darwin found that each island had a different kind of tortoise. There were also many different kinds, or *species,* of finches. Some were large and some were small. They had different songs. Their beaks were shaped differently, too. Darwin wondered why one kind of bird needed so many different kinds of beaks. He wondered how they had all changed.

He watched them closely, and he saw that each species ate a different kind of food. On some islands one kind of finch ate flowers and plants. On another island another kind of finch ate insects. Some ate only large seeds, and some ate only tiny seeds. Darwin wondered why.

Darwin stayed in the Galápagos only five weeks. When he returned to England he thought about what he had seen. He studied the specimens he had collected. He came to believe that plants and animals were able to change, or *evolve*.

The beaks of the finches had evolved so they could eat the food that was most available on the island where they lived. Many species of animals had evolved into new and separate species. Darwin wrote about these ideas in a book called *The Origin of Species*. All over the world scientists still study this remarkable book.

THE DESERT IN THE SEA

Most of the islands are desert surrounded by water. For months little rain falls. When it does fall, the volcanic rock and soil quickly soak it away. Only one island, San Cristóbal, has a stream of fresh water that flows all year round.

FUN FACT Water is so scarce that goats drink seawater. Doves drink drops of water that form from the steam around fumaroles.

The islands have two seasons. From June to December, cooler waters flow around the islands. The air over these waters is heavy with drizzle and mist. The sky is often cloudy, the sea choppy, and the winds blow cold. This is the *garúa* season. "Garúa" is the Spanish word for drizzle. But most of the islands remain dry. This is known as the dry season.

At this time a layer of mist lies over the ocean. The wind carries this mist toward the islands. The higher parts of the islands catch the mist, which then turns to drizzle and dampens the earth. The lower parts of the islands stay dry. But trees and plants high on the volcanic slopes soak up the water.

From January to May warmer waters flow south from the Gulf of Panama. These warm waters come to the islands from Christmastime to May. They are called the *El Niño* current. Now the air is warm, the sky usually clear.

Some years El Niño flows far south down along the coast of Peru. Some years it never even reaches the Galápagos. But when it does, heavy rains and thunderstorms drench the coast and the highlands. This is the rainy season for all the islands. Flowers blossom, desert trees and shrubs brighten with green. Land birds lay their eggs with the first rain and hatch their young as the insects emerge.

The warm currents bring rain and life to some creatures. But they may also bring hunger and death to others. If El Niño warms the waters for too long, the fish cannot live. When the fish disappear, seals and sea lions die of starvation. Sea birds abandon their young because there is no food to give them.

GIANT CACTI AND SUNFLOWER TREES

Some islands of the Galápagos crouch close to the sea. On these islands only dry, desert plants grow. Some islands tower into the clouds, catching the garúa moisture. On the higher islands, the land grows greener as it rises.

Mangrove trees grow tangled roots along beaches and in sheltered

On Bartolomé Island, shrubs and cacti grow right on the beach.

bays. These trees thrive in salt water. Pelicans, frigate birds, and herons build their nests among the shiny green leaves. Sea turtles and sharks swim in the waters of the mangrove lagoons. Brown noddy birds perch on the backs and necks of feeding pelicans. They wait to catch scraps of fish that fall out of the pelicans' bills. Saltbush and other plants that can stand the salty water grow along the shores and sandy dunes. Vines of beach morning glories lift their bright blossoms to the sun.

FUN FACT David Porter of the *Essex* wrote (c. 1814) that his crew stewed the juice of the prickly pear cactus fruit with sugar to make a delicious syrup. They used the skins of the fruit for preserves in pies and tarts.

Sea lions lounge under the sparse shade of a prickly pear cactus.

Away from the beaches the land is dry and desertlike. Here palo santo trees grow. Their name in Spanish means "holy stick." Their tiny white flowers have almost no smell, but the twigs of the tree give off a sharp scent when broken. During the dry season palo santo trees drop all their leaves. Forests of pale, bare branches wait for the rain that will turn them green.

Throughout the dry areas cacti grow. Their thick stems and pads store water from the rainy season. Lava cacti, which look like short cactus posts, grow close to the ground.

Prickly pear cacti may grow to 30 feet tall. Orange bark covers their thick trunks. Prickly spines poke from their green pads. The Galápagos Islands are the only place in the world where these cacti grow into trees. Tortoises and land iguanas eat the pads. Doves and mockingbirds eat the fruits. Finches eat the seeds, flowers, and fruits. These animals help to spread the seeds so that more will grow.

Higher up on the larger islands, small trees and tangled shrubs grow. Gradually the moist, shady forests take over. Where the garúa mists hang over the hillsides, Scalesia trees crowd together. These trees are relatives of sunflowers and daisies. Green umbrellas of leaves with small white flowers hang overhead. Vines and moss hang from the trees, and shrubs grow near the ground. These forests stay green all year round.

On the very tops of some islands, ferns and grasslands grow. Short-eared owls hunt for small birds and rats in the tall grass. In potholes and ravines, ferns grow into nine foot tall trees. They lift long, lacy fronds to the light.

"WALKING STONES"

Millions of years ago giant tortoises lived in North and South America. But they died out. The only giant tortoises found in nature live on the Galápagos Islands and on an island in the Indian Ocean.

How did they get to the islands? Maybe a few young tortoises rode on rafts of plants and trees. Maybe smaller varieties floated to the islands and evolved into giant tortoises. However they came, they found islands where they had no enemies.

Tortoises of the Galápagos eat cacti, grass, and shrubs.

On islands where plants grow close to the ground, tortoises have dome-shaped shells. On drier islands, where the ground is barer and cacti grow tall, tortoises have shells that are high in front, like a Spanish saddle. This allows them to stretch their necks up higher to reach food. These saddle-backed tortoises also have longer necks and legs.

Tortoises live for many years. Crawling slowly, they search for food and water. Rainwater collects in hollows in the rocks. Tortoises gather at these spots when it rains. In some places on the islands, they have worn the rough lava into smooth paths leading to these watering places.

In the cooler morning and evening tortoises browse on cacti, grass, and shrubs. At night they sleep in pools or muddy wallows if they can find them. In the wet season they mate. The females lay their

FUN FACT Hawks sometimes perch on the shells of tortoises. From there they watch for their prey.

eggs in soft dirt. When the eggs hatch, tiny tortoises must make their way out of the ground and survive on their own.

By the time they are 20 years old, tortoises are large. But they can live much longer. Records show that at least one tortoise lived to be 100 years old. If a tortoise is not killed by people or by falling into a crack in the lava, it may one day just stop moving. It may stay in one place for months, waiting to die.

SEA DRAGONS

What is four feet long, has green legs, has patches of red, black, and green on its body, looks like a small, ferocious dragon, and spits salt water? If you guessed a marine iguana, you are right.

The marine iguana lives on the barren lava edges of some islands. It is the only iguana in the world that eats seaweed. When the tide is

The marine iguana makes its home on some of the Galápagos Islands.

low, it crawls among the rocks in the surf and chomps away. Some swim out into the ocean and dive down 20 or 30 feet to graze on the seaweed growing on rocks down there.

When it has finished feeding, the marine iguana comes back on land. It finds its way to its own territory by licking the rock with its large, red, fleshy tongue. Its sense of smell is in the tongue.

The marine iguana drinks seawater. The glands near its eyes collect salt from the water. When disturbed, it shoots a spray of salty water through its nostrils.

Marine iguanas look ferocious because of the shape of their head and dragonlike crest. But scientists say marine iguanas are gentle creatures. They will not scratch or bite like the land iguana. Their skin is quite soft. Even the crest of spikes that runs from their heads to the tips of their tails are harmless. They are not afraid of people. If a person comes near, they will simply move aside.

One species is brightly colored with red and green and black patches. Others are mostly gray or black.

Marine iguanas have black staring eyes and long claws. Those claws are needed to cling to the rocks in the turbulent sea where they feed.

They collect in groups of up to thousands. Marine iguanas stand for hours in the sun. They are storing heat and energy for their next feeding spree. They swim in cold water, so they often eat when the tide is low to save body heat. The black lava rocks they lie on get very hot. Iguanas have learned to position their bodies in ways to keep from overheating.

Iguanas have been described as hideous, imps of darkness, and monsters-in-miniature. Despite all those awful-sounding names, they have managed to adapt beautifully and thrive on the stark, bare lava of the islands.

THE CHILLY TROPICS

Along the western edges of Fernandina and Isabela, cool water wells up from deep in the ocean. This water is rich with food. Fish thrive. Penguins, seals, and sea lions feast on the fish.

FUN FACT At night marine iguanas may stack themselves on top of one another to keep warm.

Sea lions inhabit the cool waters off Fernandina and Isabela.

One of the smallest penguins in the world nests along the rocky shores of Fernandina and Isabela. Galápagos penguins are only about 14 inches high. On shore they waddle clumsily. They cannot fly through the air. But in the ocean they use their wings to fly through the water. They are the only penguins to live in the heat of the tropics. The cold waters along these islands help them survive.

Fur seals, too, are animals that usually live in cold climates. Much of the day they hide from the hot sun in the shade of rocks and caves. At night they swim in the cool western waters, hunting for fish and octopuses.

Flightless cormorants catch fish along these islands. These furry-looking birds have long, snaky necks, powerful beaks, and short, stubby wings. The first cormorants who came to the islands could fly

A female frigate bird keeps a watchful eye out for predators as she protects her chick.

like other cormorants. But in the Galápagos they had no enemies to fly from. Many scientists believe that slowly, over thousands of years, their wings became smaller and smaller. Gradually their wings became too small for flying.

Their bodies became more streamlined for swimming. When they swim they tuck their wings in tight and use their large webbed feet. When they come out of the water, they stretch their ragged wings out in the sun to dry. They are the only flightless cormorants in the world.

The Galápagos Islands are home to many kinds of birds, including the oyster catcher, which uses its long beak to crack open clams.

ISLANDS OF BIRDS

The Galápagos are a land of seabirds. Clouds of petrels flit in the sky. Boobies scream. Mockingbirds and finches are everywhere. Mockingbirds are so fearless they will walk right over people's feet or try to untie their shoelaces. A few flamingoes nest in the islands. Stalking on long legs in salty marshes, they eat the tiny pink shrimp that give them their color.

Genovesa is a dry, rocky island. But it is home to the largest colonies of seagoing birds in the Galápagos. Thousands of red-footed boobies build their nests of twigs. Frigate birds fly after the boobies to rob them of their fish. Storm petrels nest under the lava crusts.

On Española, a small island on the southeastern edge of the Galápagos, 40,000 waved albatrosses come to nest. This large white seabird has gray wavy lines on its chest. It spends most of its life flying over the open sea, hunting for food. But each year some of these birds return to Española to breed.

They arrive in March and perform their mating dances, swaying and pointing their beaks, calling with long "whoo-oooos." Each pair of birds lays one large egg on the rocks.

When the chicks are old enough to feed themselves, the birds wing off again across the water. They will not return to land until it is time to breed again. Then, across miles of the vast Pacific Ocean, they will find their way back to the shores of the small island.

DARWIN'S FINCHES

There are 13 different kinds of finches in the Galápagos. Finches live on almost all the islands. In the wet season they eat mainly caterpillars. But when the long dry season comes, they must find other food or die.

Some finches are special companions to the land iguanas. A land iguana rises up on all four legs so it is off the ground. A finch hops on its back and begins searching for ticks.

Finches also eat the blood-filled ticks off the long necks of the Galápagos tortoises.

Another finch builds its nest in a cactus tree. Its beak is thick at the base and long and pointed. As it feeds deep in the flower its head becomes covered with pollen. It also eats the yellow flower and fruit of the cactus. Since its beak is not quite long enough, it will drill a little hole at the base of the flower or fruit. From this hole the finch drinks the sweet nectar and eats the soft seeds.

The Galápagos Islands have a rare bird called the woodpecker finch. This clever fellow has learned to use a tool. In all the earth there are few animals or birds that can use tools. It holds a spine

The blue-footed booby is a magnificent diver. It can dive into the water from a height of 30 feet to catch its prey.

from a cactus in its beak and digs in soft or rotting wood until it finds a fat grub. It pokes until the grub finally wiggles out. Then the finch drops the twig and gobbles up the grub.

Some finches that live on the northern islands of Wolf and Darwin drink blood. These "vampire" finches peck at the tail feathers of the booby bird until it begins to bleed. Then they drink the blood from the wound.

The largest finch is a vegetarian. It eats flowers, fleshy fruits, leaves, buds, seeds, and even lichens.

The large ground finch has a thick, short beak. It cracks very hard seeds. The small ground finch, which has a tiny beak, eats only tiny grass seeds. There is even a medium-size finch that eats medium-size seeds. There are small, medium, and large tree finches, too.

Although most finches sing a few dull notes, the warbler finch sings a true song. It even looks and acts like a real warbler.

All these birds build round-domed nests with side openings. They lay white eggs with pink spots. Even though they have changed in color, size, and beaks, it is easy to see that they all evolved from the same ancestor thousands of years ago.

LIFE IN A CALDERA

Some volcanoes are round on top. Others have collapsed inward. This happens when the magma in the main vent withdraws and the heavy roof falls in. This forms a crater called a caldera.

The caldera floor may be covered with ash and lava. In time plants

Visitors who climb to the summit of Bartolomé Island can see for miles.

begin to grow—grass, low bushes, or cacti. It may become thick with vegetation or stay sparse like a desert.

Water may collect in lakes or mud holes. Tortoises may cool themselves in the mud. Pintail ducks swim on the lakes. Yellow-orange, four-foot-long land iguanas roam like dragons on the rim of the caldera. They gobble yellow flowers from prickly pear cacti. Lava lizards snap up flies.

No large freshwater fish swim in the lakes. No frogs croak at night. These animals never reached the islands. Yet there are dragonflies, bees, grasshoppers, spiders, moths and even some butterflies.

Hawks soar above looking for a tasty meal of baby iguana.

In the rainy season flowers bloom. In the early morning, steam from fumaroles may fill the caldera with a fine mist. Rocks may rumble and fall from eruptions along the edge. For millions of years in a quiet caldera, life goes on.

DANCE OF THE BLUE-FOOTED BOOBY

One of the most beautiful of the seabirds is the blue-footed booby. It is a large bird with dark brown feathers, a pure white breast, and brilliant blue feet.

On the flat, sandy floor of the volcano of Daphne Major Island, blue-footed boobies gather in thousands. Here they court their mates and raise their chicks.

When ready to mate, the male begins a strange dance. He points his beak to the sky and lays his wings back away from his breast. He struts about slowly lifting his great webbed feet. First he raises one large blue web and then the other, appealing to his mate to join him. He whistles and she honks. Soon she twines her neck with his as they continue to point at the sky.

After a bit he brings her a piece of twig. She gives him a similar gift of a pebble or a feather. They place them carefully on the ground and move them about. But these birds do not make a nest.

The mother lays two or three large white eggs on the bare ground.

A hungry blue-footed booby gets its meal right from the mouth of its parent.

Both parents take turns keeping the eggs warm. They do this by putting their huge webbed feet, filled with blood vessels, over the eggs. When the eggs hatch, one will guard the chicks while the other fishes.

Boobies are magnificent divers. They can dive-bomb into the water from 15 to 30 feet, swim under their prey, and swallow it underwater. They maintain enough speed to continue flying as they emerge from the ocean.

The chick prods its father's or its mother's throat until its beak opens. Then the chick thrusts its head deep into its parent's gullet and gulps down a meal.

There are other boobies on the islands. Red-footed boobies have blue bills and large red webbed feet. The masked booby is black and white with a yellowish beak and gray feet. It has a black "mask" across its eyes.

Frigate birds, with their wing spans of eight feet, are strong and graceful fliers.

PIRATES OF THE SKIES

Frigate birds are magnificent flyers. From tip to tip their long black wings stretch eight feet. They can glide for hours above the ocean waves.

A frigate's feathers are not waterproof, so the birds cannot dive into the sea for fish. But they fly so swiftly that they can catch flying fish in midair. They also scoop up fish from just below the surface of the water with their long, hooked beaks.

Frigates usually fish for themselves. They will also steal fish from other birds. A booby flying along with a catch of fish may find itself chased by several frigates. The frigates twist and turn, easily outflying the booby. A frigate may seize the booby's wing tip or tail with its beak. When the booby drops its catch, a frigate dives to snatch the

When attracting a mate, a male frigate bird puffs up the red skin under its throat.

food, often before it hits the water.

A male frigate bird has a bare patch of skin under his throat. To attract a mate, he perches on a shrub and fills this pouch with air. The bright red balloon puffs out to almost half the size of his body. When a female frigate bird flies over, he tilts back his head, spreads his wings to show her his pouch, and waits. If the female lands, she may choose him for a mate. She then gathers twigs for a nest. The male guards the nest from other frigate birds who try to steal the sticks.

Many animals can find food on the shores of the Galápagos Islands.

LIFE AT THE WATER'S EDGE

Rocky shores, sandy beaches, mangrove lagoons, and mud flats ring the islands. Waves crash endlessly against the rocks. Twice a day the tide rises. Where land and sea meet, many animals find food.

Lava lizards catch flies and other insects in the tidal zone when the tide is out. Birds feed on crabs and shellfish. Marine iguanas graze on seaweed. Octopuses hide in tide pools. Bright red Sally Lightfoot crabs skip across the wet rocks, and ghost crabs leave a trail of sand

FUN FACT Beaches in the Galápagos are black, brown, green, red, and orange. They come from the different colored lavas that are worn into sand. White beaches are formed from the remains of seashells and sea creatures.

balls on the beach. Four-eyed blenny fish come up from the water and hop over the sand on their tails and fins, searching for food. These fish can breathe air for as long as two hours.

Fur seals and sea lions love the rocky coast. Sea lions lie on beaches soaking up the sun. Young sea lions splash in the water. They love to body surf. They play with each other, with penguins, or with a piece of seaweed. Sometimes a sea lion will seize a marine iguana by the tail, just for fun. It will toss the iguana about, then let it go.

A bull, or male sea lion, guards each group of females and young. He swims from border to border in his territory. If he sees the fin of a shark cutting through the water, he drives the youngsters up onto shore.

A sea lion mother has one pup. When it is a week old, she leaves it to find food. When she comes back from fishing she calls out. Each pup answers only to its mother's voice. Calling back and forth, mother and pup find each other so the pup can nurse.

Chocolate-colored fur seals nurse their babies, too. With blunt faces and thick bodies they look like little bears. They keep to the rocky parts of the coast because the sand gets into their thick fur. At one time these seals were almost extinct. Now they are protected.

DANGERS AND DAMAGES

Life on the islands has its dangers. Hawks swoop down on lava lizards. Boiling lava pours suddenly out of a volcano. But the biggest threat to the islands has always been human beings and the damage they have done.

Once there were probably 250,000 giant tortoises on the islands. There were so many that early explorers claimed they could walk on the tortoises' backs without ever touching the ground. Now only about 15,000 tortoises survive. The tortoises had no natural enemies, so they had no defenses. When bothered, a tortoise simply withdraws into its shell with a hiss.

Pirates, whalers, and settlers killed the giant tortoises for their meat and oil. Scientists took tortoises for their museum collections.

Sea lions of the Galápagos like to lie on the rocky coast and soak up the sun.

Even on islands where the animals were almost extinct, scientists captured and killed many tortoises.

Fourteen different kinds of tortoises once lived on the islands. Now only 11 remain. On Floreana the tortoises disappeared over 100 years ago. On Santa Fe they are also extinct. Only one giant tortoise was ever found on Fernandina. Scientists killed it to study it. Of all the tortoises that lived on Pinta Island only one male remains. He has been nicknamed "Lonesome George."

Other animals suffered, too. They were easy prey, fearless and tame. Settlers on San Cristóbal killed all the hawks there. United States soldiers stationed on Baltra during World War II killed every land iguana on the island.

Settlers brought cattle, pigs, cats, dogs, and donkeys. Some of these animals escaped and became wild, or *feral*. Black rats probably escaped from ships that stopped at the islands. Sailors set goats free on some islands to breed. Native animals had no defenses against these newcomers.

Pigs, dogs, and black rats eat the eggs and young of tortoises, land iguanas, and birds. Cats attack birds and young iguanas. Wild donkeys and cattle trample tortoise nests.

Feral goats eat the plants that are food for tortoises and iguanas. They even chomp through the thick trunks of cactus trees until the tops fall over. Then the goats can eat the spiny pads. Cows, horses, and donkeys trample ferns and brush. The natural plants cannot survive, and grassland takes over.

SAVING THE ISLANDS

In 1959 the Galápagos Islands became a national park. Within a few years a scientific station was built on Santa Cruz. It is called the Charles Darwin Research Station. Scientists from around the world come to the islands. Their biggest concern is trying to protect the Galápagos Islands from the harm that people do. This is a big job.

People who live on the islands are helping. Many work for the national park. Others help to see that tourists do not harm animals or plants. Still others help at the research station.

On some islands hunting teams have been sent out to kill wild dogs and goats. In 1950, a fisherman left a few goats on Pinta Island. By 1970, there were 20,000 goats. It took the research station 14 years to rid the island of the goats.

Scientists are also helping to breed tortoises and land iguanas. Tortoise eggs are carried to the station in padded backpacks. They are hatched in concrete ovens warmed by the sun. The young tortoises are protected in special pens. When they are about five years old they are returned to their island homes.

All visitors to the islands must follow these rules:

Don't disturb or remove any native plants, animals, or rocks. You may not touch any living thing. On some islands you will be walking right by the nests of birds. Don't feed them. Don't follow, chase, or startle them.

You must have a qualified guide with you when you visit the islands.

Shake your clothes and shoes, and wash your shoes and feet as you leave each island. This helps make sure seeds, insects, and soil stay on the island where they belong.

Stay on the marked trails. If an animal is on the path go quietly around it.

Don't litter.

Don't buy souvenirs of native products (except wood). Don't buy sea lion teeth, black coral, or tortoise/turtle shell products.

Help care and preserve so others who come after you can see what you have seen. Be a *conservationist*.

The Galápagos Islands are in better shape today than they were 20 years ago. All the native plants and animals on the islands and in the seas around them are protected. The national park and the Darwin Research Station are working hard to help people understand their place in this fragile world.

FUN FACT Most of the islands have had more than one name. Santa Cruz Island has had eight different names.

Waves crash endlessly against the rocky shores of the Galápagos Islands.

FOR MORE PARK INFORMATION

For more information about the Galápagos Islands, write to:

Embassy of Ecuador
2535 15 Street NW
Washington, DC 20009

PARK MAP

Galápagos National Park

GLOSSARY / INDEX

BASALTIC LAVA 9—A hard, dense, dark volcanic rock often having a glassy appearance, typical of ocean volcanoes.

BUCCANEER 14, 15—The owner of a ship sent by his king to make war against another nation's ships during the 17th and 18th centuries.

CALDERA 9, 32, 33—A large crater formed when the top of a volcano collapses in on itself.

COLONIST 18—An original settler in a distant land who is still ruled by the country from which he or she came.

CONSERVATIONIST 41—A person who believes in and practices saving and protecting natural resources.

CRATER 9, 32—A bowl-shaped hollow at the mouth of a volcano.

EL NIÑO 20—A warm current that brings rain and warmer temperatures to the Galápagos starting around December.

EVOLVE 19, 32—A gradual process in which something changes into a different and usually more complex form.

EXTINCT 16, 39, 40—A species of plant or animal no longer existing in the world.

FERAL 40—A domestic animal that has gone wild.

FUMAROLE 7, 19, 33—A hole in a volcanic area from which hot smoke and gases rise.

GALLEON 15—A large ship used mainly by the Spaniards of the 15th and 16th centuries.

GARÚA 20, 23—(pronounced *gah-roo-ah*) The cool season in the Galápagos when a fine, misty drizzle falls in the taller islands, while the lower islands remain dry.

HOGSHEAD 14—A large cask that holds 63 gallons of liquid.

HOT SPOT 6—A natural break in the earth's crust out of which hot magma flows.

INCAS 13—A South American people who ruled one of the largest and richest empires in the Americas. The Spanish conquerors destroyed their civilization in the 16th and 17th centuries.

ISLET 9—A little island.

LAVA 6, 7, 9, 10, 11, 14, 17, 25, 26, 30, 32, 39—Melted rock that pours out of a volcano.

GLOSSARY / INDEX

LICHEN 10—A scaly growth, made up of fungi and algae, on rocks and trees.

MAGMA 6, 7, 32—The molten rock under the earth's crust.

MAMMALS 10—Warm-blooded animals that give birth to their young rather than lay eggs.

NATURALIST 19—A person who studies plants and animals.

NICHE 11, 12, 13—The role a plant or animal plays in its environment. This includes what it eats, where it lives, and its relationship to everything else around it.

PIRATE 15—A robber who roams the high sea.

REPTILES 10—A class of cold-blooded animals with backbones. Reptiles breathe by means of lungs and usually have skin covered with horny plates or scales.

SHIELD VOLCANO 9—A rounded volcano made up of many layers of basaltic lava.

SPECIES 19—A group of animals or plants with common traits.

SUMMIT 9, 32—The top; the highest level.

VENT 6, 7, 32—The crusted opening in a volcano from which gas and steam escape.